D1109427

The Troubles of
Queen Silver-Bell

The Troubles of Queen Silver-Bell

As Told by Queen Crosspatch

Frances Hodgson Burnett

Illustrated by
Harrison Cady

DERRYDALE BOOKS
New York • Avenel, New Jersey

This 1992 edition is published by Derrydale Books,

distributed by Outlet Book Company, Inc.,
a Random House Company,
40 Engelhard Avenue, Avenel, New Jersey 07001.

Printed and bound in the United States of America

Book design by Claire Moritz

Library of Congress Cataloging-in-Publication Data

Burnett, Frances Hodgson, 1849–1924.
The troubles of Queen Silver-Bell: as told by Queen
Crosspatch / Frances Hodgson Burnett: illustrated by Harrison
Cady.
p.   cm.
Summary: Two short stories. In the first Queen Silver-Bell
loses her temper and becomes Queen Crosspatch. In the
second a little girl is changed into a rook to hatch abandoned
eggs.
ISBN 0-517-07247-5
1. Children's stories, American. [1. Fairies—Fiction.
2. Birds—Fiction.   3. Short stories.]   I. Cady, Harrison,
1877–ill.   II. Title.
PZ7.B934Tr   1992
[Fic]—dc20   91-30558
CIP
AC

ISBN 0-517-07247-5

8   7   6   5   4   3   2   1

THE TROUBLES OF
QUEEN SILVER-BELL

I AM A FAIRY. Now I won't be contradicted; there are such things as Fairies. I am one myself and have been one ever since the beginning of the world. What is more, I am the Queen of the Fairies. I am the Queen of millions and millions and millions and millions of lovely little people, as beautiful as flowers and butterflies. They can do all the things people want to have done, and find all the things that are lost, and turn pumpkins into golden coachmen, and anything into anything else that is nicer, and *yet* as the years have gone on, until it isn't "Once upon a Time" anymore, people have grown so stupid that they don't *believe* in us and they are so blind they cannot see us even when we are dancing before them, and they cannot hear us, even when we are singing and singing to them:

> Why can't you see? Oh! if you knew
> Fairies are real—Fairies are true.
> Fairies are here—Fairies are there,
> Fairies are waiting everywhere,
> In the house and in the street,
> On your shoulder, at your feet,
> By your fire and on your book,
> If you only had the sense to look.
> Why can't you see? Oh! if you knew,
> Fairies are real—Fairies are true.

But you cannot make people *believe* it. Even children don't. That is what is the matter with everything. People will believe in nasty things and they won't believe in nice things, and that has been going on so long that my great fear is that the Fairies themselves will forget their accomplishments, and then what will become of Fairyland? Rumors have come to my palace of Fairies who were not even able to change themselves into rabbits when it was *very* important indeed, and I heard of one Fairy who was trying to turn a naughty little boy into a pussy cat because he was pulling a kitten's tail, and she only got as

2

far as the meow and the claws and she forgot how to do the rest, and he ran away m-e-owing and scratching his face with his sharp claws when he tried to rub his eyes because he was crying. But he could only cry like a cat—and it served him right. But it upset me very much to hear of it. If that sort of thing goes on, Fairies will be as ignorant as human beings and Fairyland will go to ruin. And I won't have it. I used to be called Queen Silver-Bell until lately—until the misfortune happened I am going to tell you about. I was called Queen Silver-Bell because I was always laughing in those good old days when it was "Once upon a Time." And all the Fairies said my laugh sounded just like tiny silver bells, tinkle—tinkle—tinkling. But now I am called Queen Crosspatch because I scold and scold and scold—and it all happened in this way:

You see, the most important thing in the world —whether you are a Fairy, or a little boy or a little girl, is never—never—never—never to lose your Temper. Most people don't know that a Temper is really a Fairy. And as long as you can keep him he is the cleverest and the delightfulest Fairy of all. He is always laughing and doing lovely things. He has little golden and silver shovels to dig dimples in your face and make you so pretty that people adore you and want to give you things and take you to the circus and the pantomime and to Christmas parties and sights and treats, and he has a tiny gold and pearl and ruby paint box full of the most heavenly colors, and tiny brushes to paint everything so that it looks beautiful and delightful, and he whispers songs and stories in your ear and makes you enjoy yourself and laugh all the time. *But* the minute he gets away and you lose him, he turns into a tiny black Imp Fairy and pinches and kicks you and tells lies to you and whispers ugly things to you until you are perfectly mizz'able and make everybody else mizz'able too. I had a lovely little Temper. There never was a cleverer one nor a prettier one. He was tiny and rosy and his face was pink and full of dimples, and I perfectly loved him. I always kept him in a tiny silver cage, or fastened to my waist by a diamond chain. I had nothing else I was as fond of and I would not have parted with him for anything. I can scarcely bear to think of him now he is gone.

One day I was in a garden where a lady was talking to a little girl. I had been sitting on roses and swinging on lilies and dancing on the very

A Temper is really a Fairy

flowers they were gathering and doing everything to attract their attention. But I could not make them look at me and I began to forget I was carrying the tiny silver cage with my darling little Temper in it, and suddenly the lady said to the little girl:

"Do you like stories about Fairies?"

When I heard that, it quite cheered me up, and I jumped on to the edge of a flower and began to sing:

> Silver-Bell, Queen Silver-Bell!
> What you want to know she can always tell
> If you only believe in Silver-Bell.

And what do you suppose that child said? She opened her silly blue eyes and stared like a sheep and answered:

"What is a Fairy?"

I just jumped down and screamed. I stamped my feet and shook my fists, and my golden floss silk hair flew all about, and the silver cage flew out of my hand and the door flew open and my darling little Temper burst out and darted away. And his pink face and his dimples and his silky curls and his dancing blue eyes and his tiny coat all sparkling with jewels were gone and he was changed into a vicious, ugly, black, thin, little Imp with squinting steel-colored eyes it made me ill to look at.

I rushed after him as hard as I could. He hid himself in a red nasturtium and the minute I got near him he darted into a rose bush and the thorns tore his horrid little black clothes into rags and tatters but he only grinned and made faces at me; and then he ran across the lawn and into the park, and jumped onto a fawn's back, and it was so frightened by the horrid little thing that it galloped and galloped away and I after it; and then he climbed an oak tree and swung on a big leaf making faces and I kept getting crosser and crosser and hotter and hotter and I began to call out:

> If you'll stop I'll give you a golden cage,
> If you'll stop I'll give you a richer wage.

And then because I had lost my Temper I couldn't stop myself, and I called out:

If you stop I'll give you a crack on the head.

He jumped onto a fawn's back

And he just turned round and grinned and put his tiny black thumb at the end of his tiny black nose in the most rude way and shouted at me:

> That's not so easily done as said,
> Crosspatch, Crosspatch, Crosspatch.

And just that second a skylark flew up out of the grass and he swung out on a leaf and sprang on to his back and was carried up and up and up and up—higher and higher and higher and higher into the very sky itself and I knew I had lost him, perhaps forever, and I flopped down on a buttercup and cried and scolded and scolded and cried as hard as ever I could. And the worst of it was that I couldn't stop scolding. When you have lost a darling sweet little Temper you can't stop. I was cross every minute and I frowned and scowled so that my face was all over wrinkles.

> I scolded the grass and I scolded the flowers,
> I scolded the sun and I scolded the showers,
> I scolded the castles, I scolded the towers,
> And I scolded the Fairies for hours and hours.
> When I went to my Palace I scolded the pages,
> When I sat on my throne I went into rages.
> I scolded the birds as they sang in their cages,

I was afraid I should scold on for ages and ages.
The hens that were Fairies forgot how to hatch,
The Fishermen Fairies forgot how to catch,
And the little Boy Fairies all in a batch
Called after me everywhere Queen Crosspatch.

That was what happened. And I should like to know if you can think of anything worse? I can't. And the very worst of it was that I knew I should never find my sweet, dear little pink Temper again, until I had done something that would make people—particularly children—believe in Fairies as they used to, "Once upon a Time," and save my dear Fairyland from going to ruin and melting away. If you don't believe in things they melt away. That's what happens to them. They just *melt away.* And so many things are like the little Pig who wouldn't go over the bridge—and I knew that if I could make the children believe, the believing children would make the Fairies begin to practice turning things into something nicer, and if the Fairies began to practice turning things into something nicer, Fairyland would be saved and not go to ruin, and if Fairyland was saved and did not go to ruin, I should find my dear, sweet, dimpled, pink little Temper again,

All Fairies have long, long hair—

and if I found my dear, sweet, dimpled, pink little Temper again I should not be Queen Crosspatch anymore but Queen Silver-Bell and laugh and laugh and laugh and laugh until the other Fairies would say my laughing sounded like tiny bells of silver, tinkle—tinkle—tinkling, and everything would be lovely forevermore. I wondered and wondered what I should do, and then I wondered and wondered again, and after I had wondered and wondered three times, I made up my mind that I would sit down *under my hair*. Of course I see you don't know what that means. Well it means something very important. All Fairies have long, long hair—sometimes it is gold color, sometimes it is squirrel color, and sometimes it is as black as black velvet, but it is always as fine as floss silk and can either be tucked up in a knot or hidden under a pearl cap, or allowed to float and dance about—or hide you altogether if you want to be hidden. And if you want to *think*, the best thing in the world is to sit down on the floor and shake down your hair so that it falls down to the floor, and makes a little tent all around you. I always do it when anything important is on my mind. So this time I sat down on a scarlet toadstool spotted with black, and put my head on my knees, and shook out my hair into a tent which covered me all over so that nothing but the tips of my golden shoes stuck out.

And then I sat and sat and sat, and I thought and thought and thought. And suddenly I remembered the Dormouse. Of course there was no use *my* thinking, when I could go to the Dormouse.

The Dormouse knows more than the King. Every year when the weather grows cold, the Dormouse rolls himself into a ball and he takes his hind legs and he tucks them round his ears and he doesn't move until the Spring comes. So the people think he is asleep. But he is not asleep. He is *thinking* all the time. He can think better and faster when he is rolled up and his hind legs are tucked over his ears. Perhaps everybody could. But no one ever tries it.

> He thinks of beans, and he thinks of peas,
> He thinks of bread and he thinks of cheese,
> He thinks of raisins and nuts and figs,
> He thinks of elephants and pigs
> He thinks of girls and he thinks of boys,
> He thinks of things that make a noise;
> He thinks of mice that run up stairs,
> He thinks of rabbits and of hares,
> He thinks cats should be taught to dance

The Dormouse rolls himself into a ball

And ferrets should be sent to France;
He thinks of cakes and steaks and chops,
He thinks for months and never stops.

And of course he is the best person to go to for advice. So I danced over a meadow and flew over a garden and floated over a lake and went to the Lord High Chief Dormouse of all the Dormice, who was rolled up for the winter in a warm nest at the root of a tree at the lakeside.

Then I picked up five round white pebbles and a shell and threw them one after another at his door. When I threw the first pebble I said:

This one has shaken you.

When I threw the second I said:

This is to waken you if you have fallen asleep;

When I threw the third I said:

This is to call you,

And when I threw the fourth I said:

This is to maul you till your eyes begin to peep.

And then I threw the fifth stone and the shell, and said quite crossly:

> Dormouse, come out of your house,
> Don't be proud and stiff.
> Dormouse, come out of your house,
> Or we shall have a tiff.

And then I heard him begin to grumble and to rumble and to tumble, until he tumbled out of his house and began to unroll himself out of his ball and gradually stood up on his hind legs and laid both his hands at the front of his belt and made a polite and graceful bow.

"Your Royal Highness Queen Silver-Patch," he said. "What do you want?"

He was a very polite Dormouse and he was beginning to call me Queen Silver-Bell because we had been friends before I lost my darling little pink, dimpled Temper, but suddenly he remembered my new name was Queen Crosspatch so he called me Queen Silver-Patch and I really liked it better.

"Can you spare me an hour from your winter thinking?" I said, "I want to ask your advice because you are so clever."

So I danced over a meadow and flew over a
garden and floated over a lake

He was quite pleased and he smiled and pulled down his belt and his mouth curled up at the corners.

"Well of course," he said, "you are very complimentary but when a person tucks his hind legs over his ears and thinks for six months he must think something."

"Of course," I said, and I looked at him in my sweetest way and smiled. "That is why I have brought my troubles to you."

"Dear! Dear!" he said, "and a Queen too." And he sat down by me and took hold of my hand and patted it. "What a darling teensy, teenty, weenty hand," he said, and he gave it a squeeze.

"Oh! if you will help me!" I said, looking at him as if he was the only Dormouse in the world.

"I will, I will," he answered and he began to settle his collar quite as if he was delighted.

And so I told him the whole story from beginning to end: how things had got worse and worse until it seemed as if Fairyland would fall to ruin and melt away and all my Fairies would melt away because no one believed in them and I should melt away myself—and if I could do something to make people believe, the Fairies would begin to practice their accomplishments, and if the Fairies began to practice their accomplishments, Fairyland would not go to ruin, and if Fairyland did not go to ruin, I should find my darling, plump, pink, dimpled little Temper again, and if I found my darling, plump, pink, dimpled little Temper again, I should be called Queen Silver-Bell once more, and if I was called Queen Silver-Bell again I should not be called Queen Crosspatch, and if I was not called Queen Crosspatch I should laugh and laugh and laugh all the time, and if I laughed and laughed all the time the Fairies would think they heard tiny bells of silver tinkle—tinkle—tinkling and everything would be lovely and delightful forever and evermore.

"Well, well, well," he said, and he held his chin in his hand and smoothed it. "How very profoundly interesting."

"But you will think of a plan?" I said and this time I gave *his* hand—or rather his paw—a squeeze. He quite started and he quite blushed. In fact I was quite sure that his paw had never been squeezed even by a common Fairy and I was a Queen, which made it much grander.

"Yes, Queen Silver-Bell-Patch," he said, "I really must think of a plan," and he looked embarrassed and coughed and hemmed and hawed.

What a darling teensy, teenty, weenty hand

"What is the matter?" I asked.

"Er—would you—er—mind—er—if I roll myself up in a ball for a few minutes and tuck my hind legs over my ears? I can think so much better that way. It is not—er—becoming—but it is—er —useful."

"Oh! do roll yourself up in a ball and tuck your hind legs over your ears," I said. "You are mistaken about its not being becoming. It makes you look so intellectual."

He rolled himself up like lightning—just like lightning. I never could have believed any one could roll themselves up in a ball so quickly! My Goodness Gracious! It was just like lightning— like forked lightning! And I sat on the edge of a fern leaf and waited: I think he wanted me to see how intellectual he looked, until I should be likely to remember it, for he stayed rolled up in a ball for a long time. I didn't think much of his looks myself; I must say that I would not have let him know that for the world.

At last he began to unroll. He untucked his hind legs and he untucked his front legs and he unrolled his back. Then he just gave a jump and stood on his hind legs again and made his bow, blushing and blushing.

"Did I look very intellectual?" he said.

"I shall never forget it—never," I said, "I shall think of it and think of it and think of it." And then I said in a very soft voice, "Did you find a plan?"

"Yes," he said, smiling so that his mouth spread from one ear to the other and his eyes squinched up into nothing. "I thought of a very splendid plan."

"Oh! I knew you would because you are so clever. What is it?"

"It is this," he said. "Can you write a book?"

"Certainly," I answered. "I have never written one, but of course I can if I try."

Then he rubbed his chin and looked at me out of the corners of his eyes in a very queer way.

"You are not a timid person, are you?" he said.

"No," I replied. "I am not. Besides, if I have not written books myself, I have taught other people to write them. I know a Respectable Person— *quite* a Respectable Person. She sits in a garden full of roses and any number of birds call on her and she writes books for a living, and she learned it all from me. She was apprenticed to me the minute she was born and with my help she has made quite a decent living and earned any number of roses and all sorts of flowers. And when she writes I just sit on her shoulder and whisper to her. She is really my A—manu—en—sis. Do you know what that means? It's a long word. If it's too long for you I'll explain it."

"It's a leetle too long," the Dormouse said, "though not much."

"It means a person who writes what you order him to write."

The Dormouse clapped his paws together.

"Why, that's the very thing," he said. "You see, just now I thought in the front of my head and I thought in the back of my head and when I was thinking in the back of my head I suddenly remembered that when people who are not Fairies want to persuade anyone to believe in anything they always write books about it. They write books about Lions, and books about Tigers, they write books about Africa and books about America and why should you not write books about Fairies and Fairyland and the things the Fairies do? I once lined my nest with a leaf out of a book about Dormice—though I couldn't say I slept well that winter." He put out his paw and tapped me on the shoulder several times.

"You go to that Aman-man-sis creature of

yours," he said (he couldn't pronounce the word), "and make her write thousands of books about what Fairies are doing and about how much more sense they have than people who are just People."

"It's an excellent idea," I said. Just for a moment he looked anxious.

"Can she spell?" he said. "You see there are quite a lot of people who will have spelling."

"I don't know whether she can spell or not," I answered. "But when I go to see her I will ask her and tell her she must speak the truth about it because I can't have my books spoiled just because of bad spelling. I must have Good Spelling. That is all she has to do with the matter; just to *spell* and I will do the rest."

"How do you know she is respectable?" asked the Dormouse.

"Well, I know she is because you see she was apprenticed to me and I brought her up properly. She knows about Fairies quite well and because she knows about Fairies, Animals will associate with her, and flowers. She has a pony called Amoret, and some great big horses, and when she goes into the stable in the morning they all turn round and speak to her quite as if she was an equal, besides rubbing their warm velvet noses

"Can she spell?" he said

against her. She lives in a house with a park round it and when she goes and stands on the big stone steps and calls out, 'Thistle, Thistle,' her pet donkey lifts up his head and walks slowly across the grass to her and even walks up a stone step or two just to engage in confidential conversation. No donkey would be as intimate as that with a Disrespectable Person. Animals are very aristocratic. Any number of birds know her as if they had played together in their cradles, and she has a robin who follows her about the garden and is perfectly jealous of her. He flies from one tree to another and chirps as loud as he can to try to drown the head gardener's voice when she is talking to him. Oh! yes, she's Respectable! I wish I was as sure of her spelling as I am of her respectability."

"Well," said the Dormouse, "if, when you ask her about it, you say that you don't want to frighten her, but she *must* speak the *entire* truth about it, everything may be all right."

"There's one good thing about her," I said. "She is a person who knows her place and keeps it. She won't be pushing and pretend she wrote the books herself. I will explain to her that she must sign her name as small as ever she can, and

He chirps as loud as he can

that my name must be in quite large letters, so that People will know I am the Author. I dare say she could write a little letter just to tell the children who read the books that they must not make any mistake. Of course they *are* my books and no one else's." And just at these last words I began to be a little cross and scolding again. I knew it by the hasty way in which the Dormouse began to step backward.

"Of course! Of course! Your Royal Patch-Bell-Ness!" he said hurriedly. "And if you write them of course every child with any sense will understand it, and if they read story after story written by a real Fairy they will begin to believe, and if they begin to believe, the other Fairies will begin to practice turning themselves into rabbits and guinea pigs and all sorts of nice things, and if the other Fairies begin to practice turning themselves into rabbits and guinea pigs and all sorts of nice things, Fairyland will be saved and will not go to ruin, and if Fairyland is saved and does not go to ruin, you will find your sweet little, pink little, plump little, dimpled little Temper again, and if you find you find your sweet little, pink little, plump little, dimpled little Temper again, you will not be called Queen Crosspatch, but Queen Sil-

ver-Bell and you will laugh and laugh and laugh
until all the other Fairies think they hear tiny
bells made of silver, tinkle—tinkle—tinkling, and
everything will be lovely forever and evermore."
And the thought of that pleased me so much that
I forgot I had begun to feel cross and scolding and
I jumped up and squeezed the Dormouse's paw
until he blushed crimson scarlet. Then I made
him a deep curtsey and walked away backward
just as courtiers walk backward away from the
King when they have been talking to him. And I
said in my politest way:

> Oh! I thank you, Lord High Dormouse,
> I thank you very much
> In Spanish, French and German,
> In Danish and in Dutch.

And then I whirled round and flew away as fast
as I could to find the Respectable Person and ask
her if she could spell and explain things to her.

When you see a book by me you will always see
a picture of me hidden away somewhere and you
had better look for it. One thing is certain, that
though you may have heard of Fairies you have
never read stories written by a real one. And that
is what is going to happen to you.

A Fairy is going to write a book and its name is going to be "How Winnie Hatched the Little Rooks."

Now please to remember that it is a Fairy who writes this story—a real Fairy—just as real as you are yourself—because if you DON'T remember it will make me scold like anything.

Then I made him a deep curtsey

HOW WINNIE HATCHED
THE LITTLE ROOKS

I AM A LITTLE cross to begin with, but I believe I shall get better as I go on with my story about Winnie and the little rooks, because it is such a nice story. You will scarcely believe what a nice story it is. But I feel cross because just as I was passing through the Crystal Hall in my palace to go to Rose Garden and begin to write I suddenly caught sight of a tiny little ragged black creature hiding behind one of the glittering crystal chairs and kicking its legs about and dancing and giggling in the most impudent way, and I heard it cackle at me as it peeped in and out.

"He-he-he—kee-e-e-e! She thinks she is going to write a book."

And I saw it was nothing more or less than my

little Temper, the one I lost out of my silver cage, and he looked so tatteredy and raggedy and black and ugly and saucy that I am sure I should have begun to scream and stamp my feet but that I remembered quickly, that I had made up my mind to keep myself quite quiet until some day I could pounce upon him and catch him when he wasn't expecting it and just snip him into his silver cage again and shut the door. I had the silver cage with me that minute, swinging at my waist by a tiny diamond chain and the ugly little Imp caught sight of it and you should have seen him kick up his heels and shout:

> Oh! minkery—tinkery—winkery wee
> She's got her cage and she thinks she'll get me!
> Well, minkery—tinkery. We shall see.

I stopped a moment and almost stamped, but I remembered again and clinched my teeth and flounced past him, and I am glad to say that he was so frightened that he tumbled over and lay sprawling and kicking on his back.

Then I went to the Rose Garden and found the Respectable Person waiting for me and I sat down and ordered her to Spell what I told her about Winnie.

Winnie

And this is it:

Winnie was one of the nicest little girls I ever knew. She was only five and she was a round little thing. She had a round little face and round very blue eyes, and round red curls all over her head, and she had a round rosy button of a mouth, and round fat legs, and a round little body as plump as a robin redbreast's.

She lived in a big castle and her nursery was in a tower and her nurse Binny lived in it with her. She had no papa and mama and the castle really belonged to her, but she was not old enough to care about that, because she had so many other things to talk about. She cared about Binny, who was fat and had a comfortable lap and could sing songs and tell stories, and she cared about the thousands and thousands of primroses and blue-bells which grew in the park round the castle, and she cared about the deer with horns and their wives who had no horns and the little fawn children who skipped about under the trees. But most of all she cared about the birds and was always asking questions about them. One day when Winnie and Binny were walking together Binny stopped by a hedge and said:

"There is a thrush's nest with four eggs in it, in

that hedge."

"Oh! Binny!" said Winnie, "Do lift me up and let me look at it."

"No," said Binny. "If the eggs' mother saw us do it, she would go away and never sit on the eggs again, and they would starve to death."

Then Winnie dragged her away by the hand and ran as fast as her round legs would carry her. When she stopped running, her very blue eyes were rounder than ever.

"If the eggs' father was flying about and saw us, would he tell the mother?" she said all out of breath with running.

"I dare say he would," answered Binny.

"And if the eggs' aunt saw us, or their uncles or cousins, would they tell the mother and would she never sit on the eggs again and would they starve to death?"

"That's just what would happen," said Binny. So from that time, when Winnie went walking with Binny, she always turned her face quite away from the hedges for fear a mother bird would think she was looking at her eggs and would go away and leave them to starve to death.

She was always watching birds, but I think she watched the rooks most. That was because she could look out of her window in the tower and see the Rookery where they lived. Rooks are big black birds who always fly in flocks and build their nests near each other in the tops of tall trees. A great many Rooks built their nests in some trees Winnie could see from her window and she used to sit and watch them every day. In the morning when she heard them begin to say "Ca-aw! Ca-aw! Caw!" She would run to the window and call out.

"Binny! Binny! the Rooks are getting up and going to breakfast."

Then she would watch and see first one glossy black Rook come out of his nest and stand among the green leaves and shake his wings and preen his glossy black feathers with his beak. And then he would Caw! Caw! to his wife until *she* came out and sat among the leaves and smoothed out her glossy black feathers, and then they would Ca-aw! Ca-aw! Caw! to their neighbors in the other branches and then they would Caw! to the Rooks in the next tree, and the next and the next, and the Rooks would keep getting up and answering until all the trees in the Rookery were full of Rooks, all cawing as if they were talking about the weather. But Binny told Winnie they were saying things like this.

They were laughing at the idea of being
frightened of the scarecrow

"I know where there's lots to eat,
    Caw, Ca-aw, Caw!
I know where there's a field of wheat,
    Caw, Ca-aw, Caw!
The farmer sows that he may reap,
But the Scarecrow's nodding and fast asleep,
    Who cares for the Scarecrow!"

And at last they would all rise together flapping their wings and fly away over the treetops like a black cloud, and Binny said they were laughing at the idea of being frightened of the Scarecrow the farmer put in the field to keep them from stealing his wheat.

Winnie always watched them until they were out of sight and she could hear them cawing no more.

Then about sunset she liked to be at the window to watch them come home to sleep. First she would see a little black cloud in the sky and then it would come nearer and nearer, until she saw it was made of Rooks, all flying together back to their nests in the high, high old trees. Then Binny told Winnie they were saying things like:

Flying and fun and food all day,
    Caw, Ca-aw, Caw,

> Flying and fun and meat and play,
>   Caw, Ca-aw, Caw,
> We've sat on the backs of fat old sheep
> And now we've all come home to sleep,
>   High up in our treetops.

And oh! what fun it was to see them settle down for the night. What a fuss they made cawing and talking and flapping their wings. When the last of them had got into his nest with his wife, and the cawing had stopped, everything seemed so quiet that Winnie was quite ready to get into her nest and sleep as they did. She loved the Rooks because there were so many of them, and they seemed to live so near her. She used to feel as if they knew she was watching them from the tower window.

At last one day Binny said to her.

"The mother Rooks are beginning to sit on their eggs."

Winnie gave a little jump and scrambled down from the window seat.

"Then I mustn't look at them," she said, "I mustn't look at them."

"Yes, you can look at them from here," Binny answered. "They can't see you. Get up in your seat again. There's a mother on the nest in the top of that nearest tree."

Winnie scrambled back full of joy. There was a nest in the nearest tree and she could see a bit of it and Mr. Rook was sitting near it and talking to his wife.

And he said this (I told Binny and Binny told Winnie):

> Spread out my dear, tuck in your legs,
>   Caw, Ca-aw, Caw;
> Attend to your business—eggs is eggs,
>   Caw, Ca-aw, Caw;
> It's not the first time you've been told
> That if you let your eggs get cold,
> We shall have to send for the doctor.

For the next two days Winnie sat and watched and watched. She wanted to sit in the window seat all day and she asked Binny questions and questions.

Because I was so fond of her I sent some of my Fairies to push the leaves aside near Mrs. Rook's nest so that she could see better. She began to feel as if she was the eggs' mother herself and was quite anxious when Mrs. Rook went away for a minute.

Mr. Rook was sitting near it
and talking to his wife

One day when she was watching from her window she suddenly saw a boy standing beneath the tree and looking up. All at once he began to scramble up it and he scrambled very fast.

"He will frighten Mrs. Rook," cried Winnie to Binny.

"He is going to steal the eggs," said Binny.

"Run as fast as you can," Winnie said, "and tell him he mustn't—he mustn't."

Binny ran as fast as she could, but by the time she got to the foot of the tree the boy was at the top of it. Winnie saw him put out his hand and she gave a litte scream as Mrs. Rook flew up with a loud cry, and sailed away to find Mr. Rook and tell him what had happened.

"Come down! come down!" Binny called up from the foot of the tree. "How dare you touch the Rook's eggs!"

The boy looked down and was very frightened when he saw the fat nurse from the castle scolding him. He thought she might send for the village policeman and he put the eggs back and scrambled down faster than he had scrambled up. And Binny caught him and boxed his ears before he ran away.

When she went back to the nursery in the

Binny caught him and boxed his ears

tower Winnie was crying.

"Mrs. Mother Rook will never come back and the eggs will starve to death," she said.

And she sat and watched and watched, and Binny sat and watched and watched. Mrs. Rook and Mr. Rook came and flew about and cawed and talked to the other Rooks and everybody cawed and scolded, but go back to that nest Mrs. Rook would not.

"When the sun goes down they will get cold," wept Winnie. "Oh! I wish I could go and keep them warm myself." She covered her very blue eyes with her very fat hands.

"If a Fairy would only come and help me," she cried. "Nobody but a Fairy could help me."

The very minute I heard her say that I flew on to her window ledge and let her see me.

"Just look at me," I said.

"Oh! you are a Fairy!" she gasped, and then she called out, "Binny! Binny! here is a Fairy!" But Binny had gone out of the room. I did not want her interfering.

"I am glad you know a Fairy when you see one," I said. "Would you really like to sit on the nest and keep the eggs warm?"

"In the nest on the top of the tree?" said Winnie, all in a flutter.

"Yes," I answered. "Would you like to sit on them until they change into baby Rooks, and then would you like to teach them to fly?"

"Yes! Yes! Yes!" said Winnie. "But I can't fly myself, Fairy. And Binny wouldn't let me climb up the tree."

I just turned round and blew my tiny golden trumpet. I blew it once, I blew it twice, I blew it three times. And suddenly Winnie saw a flock of lovely green things she thought were butterflies. They came flying and flying. They were my Working Fairies, dressed in their green working smocks. They all stood in a row before me on the window ledge and made a bow and sang together:

> Fairies are real, Fairies are true.
> What shall we do? What shall we do?

"Get out your tools," I ordered them, "and make this young lady small enough to sit on a Rook's nest."

They took their tiny silver hammers out of their tool bags and they began to work. Their taps were so tiny that Winnie did not feel them and only laughed as they flew up and down her and worked and worked, darting about and all talking at once, so it sounded as if a whole hive of bees

They were my Working Fairies, dressed in their
green working smocks

were buzzing.

Winnie held out her hand which was covered by a swarm of them and she laughed and laughed.

"Oh! how pretty they are!" she said. "Binny! Binny! do come and see! I am covered with Fairies!"

"Hush!" I said, "and stand still. There is a great deal to be done."

Presently she began to grow smaller and smaller and in a few minutes she was quite small enough to sit on a nest.

"Now," I said, "you are ready to go."

"But what will Binny do when she misses me?" she asked.

"Binny will not know," I answered. "I am going to leave an Imitation Winnie in your place."

Then her very blue eyes grew rounder and rounder.

"Oh!" she said.

But I knew my business and I called to one of my Working Fairies:

"Tip, can you turn yourself into a little girl?" He looked ashamed of himself and wriggled.

"I'm afraid I've forgotten how, Your Majesty," he stuttered. I stamped my foot hard and called to another one.

"Nip, can you?"

He began to wriggle too and tried to slink behind the others.

"I—I—never learned, Ma-am," he stammered.

Think how disgraceful. It shows what Fairyland is coming to.

"Rip! Skip! Trip!" I called out, and they all wriggled and tried to slink because none of them could do it, and I was just going to fly into a rage and scream when a very tiny one called Kip stepped forward looking very red.

"I've been practicing three hours a day, if you please, 'm," he said.

"Then do it this minute," I commanded.

He went and stood in the middle of the room and began. He puffed and he fluffed and he puffed and he fluffed until one of his legs was round and fat like Winnie's. Then he fluffed and he puffed and he fluffed and he puffed until the other one was like it. Then he puffed and he fluffed until his body was round and plump. Then he puffled until his arms were round, and he fluffled until he had a round rosy face. Then he puffled and fluffled and huffled all at once until short red curls came out all over his head, and he had very blue eyes and a mouth like a rose button, and when he had done

But she flew straight to the Rook's nest

he stood there and looked exactly like Winnie.

"There," he panted out, "but, my word! it was hard."

"If he stays here until I come back, Binny will never know I have been away," said Winnie.

"Of course she won't," I said. "What do you suppose I made him do it for! He is the Imitation Winnie. Now we must go or the eggs will be cold."

I touched her on the shoulder and a lovely pair of wings sprang out.

"Just try flying around the room a few times," I said. She stood on her tiptoes and gave a few flaps and sailed up to the ceiling and round and round.

"How easy it is," she said. "Oh! how beautiful."

"Now fly right out of the window and we will come with you," I said, "and take you to your nest."

But when she flew to the window ledge she stopped a moment to speak to Imitation Winnie.

"Be very nice to Binny," she said, "and always say 'please.'"

She flew right out of the window and when she got outside, flying was so delightful that she felt as if she would like to fly up into the sky. But she flew straight to the Rook's nest.

It was high up in a lovely tree and when she lighted upon the branch among all the waving, rustling green leaves she laughed for joy. There were green branches below her and green branches above her and green branches all round her, and all the trees in the Rookery touched each other, and the blue sky was quite close, and there was the nest with the lovely eggs lying there waiting for her.

"I hope they are not cold, Fairy," she said, and she put her hand on them. They were not cold, but they would have been if they had waited much longer. Then she settled down in the nest like a mother bird. She spread out her little flouncy embroidered frock and fussed and fussed until nothing could have been warmer than the eggs were.

"They won't get cold now," she said. "I'll love them and love them until they think I am their real mother." All the Working Fairies crowded round in their green smocks with their little hammers and picks over their shoulders and looked at her. They kept nudging each other and smiling delightedly. They had never seen a little girl sit on a nest before.

"Good night," I said to her.

Then all the Working Fairies said:

"Good night. Good night. Good night. Good night," in low singing silvery voices, and we all flew away.

The nest was very comfortable and the eggs grew warmer and warmer, the top of the tree rocked like a cradle, the wind whispered through the branches like a nurse saying:

"Sh—sh—sh," and in the park Winnie could hear two nightingales singing. She lay and watched the stars twinkling in the blue sky above her head until her eyes closed and she fell fast asleep. When she wakened, the sun was just getting up out of a rosy cloud, and all the air seemed full of birds singing. The Rooks were cawing and flapping about and suddenly she found she could understand what they were saying.

I had not told her about it, but I had taught her Rook language in her sleep.

A very handsome, glossy, young Rook had lighted upon a branch close to her nest and was looking and looking at her. When she opened her eyes he said this:

> My goodness me! I am surprised!
>   Caw, Ca-aw, Caw,
> Till now I never realized,

Winnie could hear two nightingales singing

Caw, Ca-aw, Caw,
That lady Rooks could be pink and white,
With feathers of snow and eyes so bright,
    It really sets me fluttering.

Such a lady Rook I have never seen,
    Caw, Ca-aw, Caw;
Such a lady Rook sure has never been,
    Caw, Ca-aw, Caw;
I really can think of nothing to say
I feel so shy I could fly away.
My gracious! I hope she'll admire me.

Winnie sat up and smiled at him.

"Are you my Rook husband?" she asked.

He put his claw up to hide his blushes of joy and fluttered about on his branch.

"Are you?" said Winnie, and she pushed her flouncy little frock aside so that he could see the eggs.

"You see I am sitting," she explained, "and when I hatch, I shall be obliged to have a Rook husband to go and get things for the children to eat. Binny says that you'd be surprised to see how much they do eat. If you are not my husband will you be him?"

"Oh! Caw! May I?" said the young gentleman

I shall be obliged to have a Rook husband

Rook.

"I should like to have you very much," said Winnie. "You are a beautiful Rook. Do come close and let me stroke you. I have always wanted to stroke a Rook. But they never will let you."

The young gentleman Rook came sidling along and stood by her with his head on one side. And you never saw anything like the airs and graces he put on when Winnie stroked him. He asked to see the eggs again and Winnie showed them to him.

"Do you think I ought to wash them every morning?" she said. "Or would they take cold if I did?"

"I am afraid they would," he said. "I never was washed."

When I came with my Working Fairies to bring her a Fairy breakfast he was sailing about over her head and flapping his wings and cawing and showing off in a perfectly ridiculous manner. He actually wanted to fly at my Working Fairies and peck them away.

"Get away, green butterflies!" he cawed. "Don't bother my wife."

But I soon brought him to order.

"Green butterflies indeed!" I scolded. "They are my Fairies—and what is more you would never have seen this new kind of lady Rook if I had not brought her here. I am Queen Crosspatch —Queen Silver-Bell *as was*." He *was* frightened then. They all knew me.

"I sent him here to be company for you," I said to Winnie.

"Oh! Thank you," she said. "He is so nice. He lets me stroke him."

He was so pleased and she was so pleased that I knew I need not trouble myself about them. Every time I went to see Winnie she talked about her Rook husband, or else I found him sitting close to her cawing softly while she stroked him, or sat with her hand on his neck. He said that none of the other Rooks had such a happy home. I never saw a bird as sentimental. He said his one trouble was that he was not a nightingale, so that he could sing to her all the night while she was sitting. He tried it once, though I told him not to do it, and Winnie had to ask him to stop. She could not go to sleep herself and it made all the other Rooks in the Rookery so angry, and besides she was afraid he might waken the eggs. It was beautiful sitting on that nest, rocking softly on the treetops and looking up at the sky. All sorts of birds used to stop to talk and sing; squirrels came scuf-

STEP LIGHTLY
OR YOU'LL
WAKEN THE EGGS

HARRISON CADY

All sorts of birds used to stop to talk and sing

fling up to call and bring ready cracked nuts; and bees came and hummed and hummed about flowers and hives, and the lady Rooks who were sitting on their nests in the other branches told Winnie story after story about the lovely places they flew to when they were not busy with families.

She grew fonder and fonder of her Rook husband. He loved her so much and was so proud of her. He would have done anything for her, and he was so delighted with the eggs.

"Whenever you hear the least little tapping sound, tell me," he said, "because that will mean one is beginning to break his shell." He would scarcely go out to get things to eat, he was so afraid of being away when she hatched.

One beautiful sunny morning he was sitting near her being stroked when she gave a little jump.

"Oh! I am sure I heard a tap!"

Then she gave another little jump and said:

"Oh! I am sure I heard a crack!"

And when she pushed her flouncy little frock aside there was a baby Rook scrambling and kicking out of his shell, and in a few minutes more, another, who was perhaps a sister, both of them with nothing on but pin feathers and with their mouths wide open. Then there began to be work for Mr. Rook to do. He had to fly and fly and fly and bring food to drop into their mouths, and the more he brought the more they wanted and the wider their mouths opened and the more they squawked and cried. He worked so hard that drops of perspiration stood on his forehead, but he was so proud that he never grumbled at all.

"You *are* a good husband," Winnie said.

"But just think how patiently you have sat on them," he answered smiling at her with his head on one side. I can tell you they both had to work before the baby Rooks were fledged. They were restless, kicking babies, and Winnie had to fuss and fuss and tuck them every few minutes to keep them from falling out of the nest and tumbling from the treetop. I used to send a guard of my Working Fairies to stand round the nest and help her. Every morning at six o'clock I used to go to see her and give her good advice.

"Make Mr. Rook peck them if they won't behave themselves," I said to her.

But she spoiled them dreadfully.

"Oh! no!" she would say. "They are so little and they have no feathers yet." And she would fuss and fuss and spread her flouncy little frock out and cover them up as if they had been little golden Rooks instead of squawky little things with big mouths and bare backs. But she was so glad that she had saved them from being starved to death that she even thought they were pretty.

One morning I went and found her in a great flutter. The baby Rooks were fledged and Mr. Rook had told her they must be taught to fly. But when he made them come out and stand on a tree they were so frightened that they would not stir and even tried to scuffle back into the nest under Winnie's flouncy little frock.

"Oh! do you think they are big enough?" she said. "Suppose they should fall from the treetop."

"If they fall they will begin to flap their wings, if they flap their wings they will find out they can fly," said Mr. Rook. "I think I'll give the eldest a little push."

"Oh! don't!" cried Winnie.

So he talked to them and argued and flew about to show them how to use their wings and he said:

Come off the tree you silly things,
    Caw, Ca-aw, Caw.
The only way to use your wings,

Caw, Ca-aw, Caw,
Is to *know* that you were made to fly
And then flap and sail into the sky,
For that's all there is in flying.

But they shivered and squawked and clung to Winnie until I began to scold them. And after I had scolded them I just marched up to the eldest one and gave him a push myself. He gave a big squawk and tumbled and his brother tumbled after him, for I gave him a push too. And of course the minute they found themselves falling, they began to flutter and flap their wings, and they found out they could fly and they just fluttered and flapped gently to the ground at the foot of their tree, and there they stood squawking and cawing and boasting to each other about their cleverness, and saying they knew they could do it. Mr. Rook flew down to them of course and Winnie was left alone.

"Oh!" she cried. "The nest feels so empty. Will they never come back?"

"They will never come back to stay," I answered. "But I will make them come and visit you on your tower window ledge. And I am sure Mr. Rook would visit you whether I made him or not."

They began to flutter and flap their wings

"Well I did hatch them, didn't I?" said Winnie. "and they didn't starve to death, and I am very fond of Binny—very."

The next evening after Binny had gone to bed, I took her back. She kissed Mr. Rook a good many times and he told her he would come to see her three times a day.

When we flew into the nursery window, Imitation Winnie was in bed waiting for us and was very glad to see us. She wanted to turn into Kip again.

But the first thing was to make Winnie the right size once more—the size Binny was accustomed to. So my Working Fairies began. They swarmed all over her like bees and began to pull and tap and puffle her out—and in a few minutes there she was standing quite big enough to put on Imitation Winnie's nightgown and get into Imitation Winnie's bed, so that Binny would find her all right when she came in the next morning.

"Oh! it has been nice," said Winnie as she cuddled down into her frilled pillow. "I never shall forget how lovely it is to rock in a nest in a treetop."

When she told Binny about it Binny believed she had been dreaming. Of course she had never

The Rooks at the nursery window

known she had been away because Imitation Winnie had looked exactly like her and had always said "please."

But there was one thing she could never understand and that was why so many Rooks used to come and fly about the nursery window and sit on the window ledge. They actually seemed to love Winnie, particularly one very glossy handsome young gentleman Rook, who called there three times a day and was so tame that he used to perch on her shoulder or stand quite still with his head on one side while she stroked him.

So, you see, that is the story of *one* of the things that would never have happened if Fairies had not been real and much cleverer than People.

The next story I am going to write is about two dolls' houses and the doll families who lived in them—and I know both families well. One doll's house was a grand one and one was a shabby, disreputable one. And one doll family I liked, and the other doll family I didn't like. And you will have to read the story and find out for yourself— if you have sense enough—which was the nice one.

Queen Crosspatch